# tricks and treats

## libby scores

Tricks and Treats by Libby Scores

Copyright: © 2025 by Elizabeth Scozzari

All rights reserved. No part of this publication may be reproduced, distributed, or transmitted in any form or by any means, including photocopying, recording, or other electronic or mechanical methods, without the prior written permission of the publisher, except as permitted by U.S. copyright law. For permission requests, contact elizabethscozzariauthor@gmail.com.

The story, all names, characters, and incidents portrayed in this production are fictitious. No identification with actual persons (living or deceased), places, buildings, and products is intended or should be inferred.

Book Cover Designed by Elizabeth Scozzari

Formatting: Deliciously Dark Editing

First Edition 2025

ISBN. 979-8-9987816-8-1

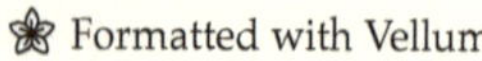 Formatted with Vellum

# content warning

Disclaimer

Content warning: this novella contains material that is sexually explicit and graphic in nature and might prove controversial to certain readers. All depictions of sexual activity are between consenting adults over the age of 18.

Happy Halloween, ghouls 🖤
I hope you get your _fill_ of extra treats this year!

# one



"I LOVE FALL!" I shout into the phone.

"I know you do, baby."

Kris' gruff voice rumbles with laughter sending a jolt to my center.

"Almost as much as I love your voice," I say.

"Wet for me already?" He asks.

We don't have to be in the same time zone for him to know this about me. The way my body has always reacted to him has been a betrayal of my emotions. Also one of the hottest things about our relationship.

It'd be hotter if I wasn't sitting on my parents' couch waiting for everyone to be ready.

"Don't start, I'm home, remember?"

"Thought you were handing out the candy?"

"I am." I sigh and roll my head back over the edge of the

couch to make sure I'm alone. "They're still putting on their costumes."

"All of them?"

I pull the phone away from my face and slide my hand up my t-shirt. I can't take a video while talking—Christmas magic has its limitations—but I take a bunch of photos, flash on, as I explain, "All of the parents are dressing up, not just mine. Thankfully or Bastian would have shit a brick, and I'd have to be hoofing it around town." I situate myself and flip through the pictures talking, hoping Kris isn't answering since I can't really hear him. Rude, but worth the payoff when I find a suitable picture. The light glints perfectly off the metal of my piercing Kris did a few months ago. "They're each going as a rockstar couple. Pretty sure Susan and Dad are going as Stevie Nicks and Lindsey Buckingham."

I press send and put the phone back to my ear.

"But don't they hate each other?"

"It depends on the decade I think," I say. "I suggested Sid and Nancy—"

"Sabby!"

"—but one of the other parents are doing it."

"It all sounds ominous," Kris says.

"Maybe," I say. "But you've seen how much they love each other."

"I still think I heard it once too."

"Gross." I laugh, and find the clicker.

"So other than doling out candy, what are your big plans?"

I turn on the TV and start to scroll through the suggested scary movies.

"Scary movie with popcorn—"

"That's not all you're eating, right?"

"—before Emma comes over with pizza and wine."

"Oh boy, at least there's pizza," he says.

"Bastian is sleeping by a friend's and Dad is surprising Susan with a hotel night." I look back over the couch and whisper, "Massage appointment in the morning after breakfast."

"Go, Ottavio!"

"Ever since Easter he's doubled down on his efforts."

"Just cause you're married doesn't mean you stop dating," Kris said.

"I'll hold you to that Kringle." I chuckle, and hear a beep through my phone. "Hold on," I say. "Emma texted me."

I open my messages and something between a groan and a laugh escapes my throat.

"What's that fallen angel up to?"

I shake my head, not that Kris can see it. Ever since I told him Emma's dating a man named Errol he keeps calling her an angel. I haven't asked him why yet, but I have a feeling there's more to my friend's god-like boyfriend that she's letting on—or even knows. I sigh and read the text out loud:

Happy Halloween! Slight delays on my end but I'm coming (not why'll I'll be late). Get your ass in a hot shower and expect a whole bunch of trickery and treats for our girls night! 🖤 🖤 🖤

"What do you think she's up to?" He asks.

"Nothing good," I say.

"It sounds like she's looking out for you."

My shoulders drop. I know he's right. Emma just wants me to have the best Halloween ever. When I started dating the son of Santa, geographical considerations were on the bottom of my list, I finally have the man of my dreams with none of the perks. Kris is great, he's amazing. But Emma has Errol, and I have a long-long-long distance relationship with a man who is insanely busy all of Q4, and most of Q3 and Q1.

"Sabby?" My head pops up. There's an echo as if—I jump as hands slide down my shoulder. A wintery pine scent tickles my nose. I turn to feel his breath on my cheek. "Trick or treat."

I drop the phone and twist so my front is pressed against the couch. Kris is leaning over, his arms pulling me into a hug.

"Happy Halloween."

He mumbles the words against my lips.

I squeal and flail about I'm standing on the couch. He picks me up, I can feel his finger tips digging into my ass. He captures my moan with his mouth. Then I heard the clamoring of feet coming down the stairs.

"Sabby?" Susan's voice calls. "You downstairs?"

Kris puts me down and I force my eyes to look anywhere other than the bulge in his pants. My whole family, including my little brother, barrel into the living room.

"Kris!"

"Woah, a superhero knows my name!" He says as Bastian barrels at him.

"It's me!" My little brother thrusts his arm out at my boyfriend and they exchange a flurry of fist bumps and slaps. When they're done, Kris says, "I thought you were really the web spinner."

"He's not *real* you know."

My brother is matter-of-fact about such things. If he knew who Kris' dad was he'd be changing his tune real quick, no matter what his friends say about "what's real or not." Since the new school year started Bastian's suspension of disbelief has been going down faster than—I blush at the thought.

"Maybe not the comic version," Kris says.

He drops to one knee, somehow still taller than me, I look over at my parents. My dad is watching Kris, but Susan's eyes are locked on me. I roll my eyes and start to smile. *Yes, it is cute.* Whatever he says to my brother has him practically vibrating in place.

My brother turns to me and something cold and slick hits my face. I scream while everyone else is laughing. I wipe away the sticky substance. It's like a slime version of a web.

"Sick!" Bastian shouts running off toward the door. "Come on guys! I'm going to get all my friends next!"

"Wait on the front yard!" My dad calls after him.

Kris stands up, and using his shirt, cleans up the rest of my face. Kissing my head he adds, "Sorry, Sabby. I didn't think he'd go for you first."

"All those siblings and no sisters, I supposed," Susan adds.

"That was cool!" My dad says walking over. "Hey Kris."

"Sir," he nods, shaking my dad's hand. His tattooed skin looks funny in a business-like handshake with my dad. He lets go, and gives Susan a hug. "You both look bad!"

"Kris," I say.

My dad laughs. "He gets it!"

"Inform us younger generations then," Susan adds.

"You remember back in the day bad meant good," my dad says.

The two of them start talking as Susan walks over to me. Her sheer black overcoat is flowing out behind her revealing a black pleasant top and black jeans. Her black top hat pops against her strawberry blonde hair. She looks amazing.

"One day, you'll have to give me his full story. But for now," she looks over her shoulder, "How old is he?" I try to see Kris from her perspective, when they hugged earlier they looked to be the same age. The way he's talking to my dad now—even with his purple v-neck t-shirt and curly wig—makes *them* look closer in age. I wonder if it's something magical in his bloodline, or if I really do have a thing for hot, older men. "You did ask, right?"

I open my mouth and then close it. "I—uh—well."

Susan sighs. "There's no judgement here Sabby, but it's been almost a year. You do know things about him." My cheeks warm and I'm sure they're as red as the velvety boxers I've seen slung low on Kris' hips. *Not now imagination.* "Other than—" Susan breathes out. "Come on my beautiful, little Rhiannon."

"Two of my three favorite people!" My dad opens his arms wide, scooping us both to his sides.

Kris snaps a photo of all of us.

"Now just you two," I say.

My parents look amazing. I take a few pictures from various

angles and drop my phone when Susan asks, "Kris, how old are you?"

His laugh echoes around the room, giving 100% future Santa. I, on the other hand, have just died a little. Looking at the picture my phone took as it fell to the floor, my dad is also in shock. Or was, I can't make eye contact with either of them.

"It depends on who you ask," he says. I hear Susan scowl. She's not fucking around. "35 or 36. I'm one of fourteen and the older ones swear my mom started jumbling us up."

The relief washes over my parent's faces. I watch as my dad squeezes Susan's shoulder before taking her hand. "Come on dear, I'm starting to hear the culmination of pre-teen boys out front." He takes a few steps forward, but Susan doesn't budge.

"Kris, before you head home, make sure you leave a list of dates for a family dinner on the kitchen counter. It'll be good for us to all get to know each other. Make sure to note any food preferences or allergies."

If I had balls they would have crawled inside my body. I look at Kris, still smiling, cool as a cucumber. He dips his head, "of course." My dad hugs me goodbye, pats Kris on the shoulder and makes his way to the door.

Susan hugs me. Her words are soft in my ear, "Being hot isn't enough, not for my girl."

The pang in my chest hits hard enough to bring tears to my eyes.

"I love you," I whisper back.

"Kris," she says, swapping me out for his larger form. "Both of you behave," she adds walking toward my dad, who is now waiting at the front door—a mix of pride and amusement etched on his face. "But not too much."

She winks as she and my dad exit into the night laughing.

Now it's my turn to be stunned.

"She's pretty cool," Kris says.

"And she's happily married, so don't get any ideas."

"Oh I have ideas," he says, wrapping his arms around me. "But none of them involve Susan."

"Even though you guys are almost the same age."

His grip tightens around me. I'm giggling as he's carrying me to the kitchen, where he sits us both on a stool. I shift my weight across his thighs and lean into his chest.

"We're not," he says.

"But you just said—"

"You know how people convert dog's ages into human years?" He asks.

"It's similar in the North Pole."

"You are a dog," I say.

"Bark, bark." He rolls his eyes and licks my cheek. "I'm probably older than both of your parents, Sabby."

My body stills. His age hadn't really meant anything before, but hearing the words. My breath catches, and before I can stop the question it tumbles out, "If time moves different, is your birthday the same here as it is home?"

He laughs and I feel it all throughout my body. Before he can answer the doorbell rings. A few kids chime "TRICK OR TREAT."

"Aren't they supposed to wait until you open the door?" Kris asks.

We stand and walk across the house. On our porch is my brother, all of his friends, my parents, plus Sid and Nancy holding up their bags. Four of Bastian's friends are covered in the webbing. Some of them are plastic, others are pillow cases, one of them has some kind of fancy-pants candy collector—I drop candy in everyone's bag giving an extra piece to the parents.

"Have fun you hooligans," I say waving them off.

"You too, kids!" Susan calls back.

She and Nancy are already linked arm in arm passing a thermos back and forth.

"I love whatever has gotten into her," I say.

"Pretty sure it's your old man."

"Come on *old man*," I say. "You said you had ideas and since Emma is going to be very late—did you two plan this?"

He closes the door and leads me into the living room.

"Scary movies, pizza, and trick-or-treaters," he says. "For now." He winks and I feel myself melt. "Everything else later."

He nips my ear as he passes into the kitchen. He returns with hot slices of pizza, garlic knots, and a smile that would make me forget he could be as old as the damn dinosaurs.

# two

A Lesson in History
Sabby

Ten o'clock rolls around and it's only the older kids running around town. I'm in my room looking at the straps of clothing on my bed. Kris and Errol are downstairs monitoring the door just in case there's any late night kiddos.

"What is this?" I ask Emma lifting the leathery straps.

She sighs. Even without turning around I know the look I'm getting.

"Warrior princess!"

Emma turns my body so I'm facing her. She's in a sheer piece of purple and pink fabric that's been strategically draped around her. It's not modest, but I can't see her areoles, so there's that.

"Which ties into Cupid and Psyche, how?"

"Technically, it doesn't." Emma tugs my t-shirt over my head. Her eyes go right to my nipples, and she laughs. "But in the tv show—"

"From the 1990s."

She reaches for my shorts and I scoot back landing on the bed.

"She and Hercules dated. And Hercules is from the same realm as Cupid."

"Except that you're mixing Greek and Roman mythology." Emma grabs my shorts, yanking them down. "OW!"

"Thank God you're cleaned up." She groans and points to the pile next to me. "Don't make me wrangle you into that. It'll be hard enough painting your face if you don't cooperate."

It's clear my opinion means nothing here. I love Halloween, but I had no plans outside of bumming it. I'm excited that she's doing this, even if I'm skeptical of the costume.

"Alright!" I say, holding my hands up. "I'll put it on."

"Win!" She goes back to futzing with her makeup. "And it's all the same. Greek, Roman." I stand and look up at her. "Same people, different names. Errol's family still practices the old ways."

"Like before the first century?" The leather lined metal feels nice against my skin. I'm surprised at how well it fits. Then I think of Kris—the replica of my shirt from earlier in the summer, the Elven magic he used to pierce my nipples. "Did Kris help with this?"

"No, I can fit your outfits, just as good as mine." She looks over her shoulder, "And yes, before 1 AD."

There's something in her face as she says it. The light in her eyes sparks like a fire is burning in there.

I continue getting dressed.

"You said you had a good time with his parents," I say, letting the comment sit.

The bralette made of more metal and lining slides up over my skin. The leather is so soft, it feels like butterfly kisses. Emma's frozen by the mirror. I look down at the straps. They're long and I'm not sure how to secure them.

"Here." Emma walks over and takes them from my hand. She wraps them around my body, turns me so my back is to her, before she secures them. She sighs. "I did. They're great. They just hate me."

"What?" I almost knock her off as I spin on my heel. "They can't!"

"You're right. *They* don't." She walks back to her makeshift makeup station. "His mom. Errol says she's jealous. His sister agrees. It doesn't matter. He's made it clear, but it still hurts."

"Oh, Em." I walk over and rub her back. "You're beautiful and kind. And funny! All things anyone would love, or be jealous of. Eventually she'll come around. If she doesn't, fuck her. He chose you." She sniffles and throws her arms around me. "It's not like she's some all mighty goddess herself." I hear Emma snort as she squeezes me tighter. "Come on," I say, stepping back. "Make me look like the most bad ass warrior princess."

"Thanks, Sabby." She wipes her eyes and gives me a once over. "Put the bottoms on before you forget all together. Then get your ass in this chair."

I'm pulling straps over my thighs and hips, certain that this is a heavily modified costume when there's a knock at the door.

"Delivery!" Errol's voice is unmistakable.

"Eyes closed," Emma scolds.

She opens the door. I bite my lip trying to hold in my giggle. Errol's body, something sculpted by ancient artists, is draped in a chiffon sash and strategically pinned diaper.

"And I thought my costume was reveling," I say.

"Should make for an interesting night."

Errol laughs as he extends two bottles of wine out. Emma grabs them and gives him a kiss on the cheek.

"Why?" I ask. I groan and look at Emma.

She waves the wine at me, passing off the bottles as she picks up the straps.

"Have you met your boyfriend?"

"Once or twice," I say.

Emma gives one last tug and sings, "TA-DA!" She claps and gestures at me like I'm the letter S and she's Vanna White. "Errol! Look!"

He opens his eyes, "Stunning!" I see color rise to my best friend's cheeks. Her man's eyes are locked in on her.

"Okay, Cupid." I say, clearing my throat. "You're gonna unpin your diaper."

He winks at Emma and then looks over at me.

"Yeah," he says, backing away from the door. "We're gonna need a centaur and a hydra to check your man if anyone so much as looks at you at all."

"Anyone?"

"Later, Cupid!" Emma closes the door on Errol. There's no yelps of pain so I imagine that he stepped back in time. "Sabby."

"Emma!"

"It's a Susan-sanctioned party! It'll be fun." She opens a bottle of wine, then the other. "Besides, we'll either win for group costume—yay mythology—or couples. Either way, I feel good about this."

"Of course you do," I say, taking the bottle from her. "You planned it."

She guides my butt into the chair and swaps her bottle out for a brush.

"Technicalities."

* * *

There are a dozen or so people in the living room by the time we've each finished our wine and Emma's done my makeup. My eyes land on the two men in the center of the living room, specifically the wider one whose muscles form a rippling wall. His dark hair and beard are trimmed, and when he turns to face me, the spark in his eye gets me wet.

He's even more stunning straight on. My gaze falls onto his loin cloth. I look sideways at Emma.

"Were you setting them up for a dick slip?"

"No," she says. A smile sweeps across her face, "But now that you mention it."

"Yours has the advantage," I say.

"Maybe," Emma says. "Errol's not wearing anything under there. Maybe Kris is?"

"One way to find out!" We start walking toward them. I notice the furniture has been moved creating the perfect place for dancing. "Prize?"

"Seems like everyone is going to win." She laughs. "Besides, you have an unfair advantage. You've seen Errol's."

"Only because you showed it to me!"

"Do I ask whose is bigger?"

I don't have time to answer the question as big hands lift me into the air.

"Did you even watch Xena?" Kris asks.

His voice raises my core temp, melting my internal organs. He spins me and returns me to the floor.

"I would have if Hercules looked like you," I say.

He wraps his hand around mine and brings me into the kitchen.

"Drink?"

"Yes please."

I look around the room. More people seem to be filling in. Most of them Emma and I know from high school and where she went to college. There's a few people I don't recognize due to their costumes. She wasn't wrong about us being the best-dressed. The only other one I see who could compete is a head-to-toe werewolf. Our eyes catch and I feel the hairs on my body stand up.

Kris pulls me into his side. His body is tense making his muscles hard. I tip my head up. He's staring at the wolf, who is still looking at me. The tips of his fingers are digging into my flesh. While not one for jealousy, Kris' touch is driving me wild. I hear Errol's comment from earlier.

"What's a hydra?" My breath comes out in a hoarse whisper. *Yeah, my man's hot as fuck.*

"Giant water snake with seven heads." His voice is practically a growl. "Why?"

"Seems Errol wasn't kidding when he said we'd need one to keep you in check." His head snaps in my direction. The greens of his eye are gone, hidden behind massive black pupils. "It's a good thing you're not Medusa, *Hercules*."

"Looks can't kill Ray." Kris grumbles. He bends forward and places a kiss on top of my head. I can't say for sure, but I have a feeling his eyes are elsewhere.

"Ray?" I ask. "You know each other?"

"He's friends with Errol."

"Who you met this evening?"

He moves his hands to my shoulders putting space between us. His pupils are less dilated, but there's an energy to him that is dampening my leathers.

"We've actually met before. Long story for another night," he says, handing me a drink. "Right now we celebrate you and the BERs."

"The brrrs?"

"Your favorite time of the year, Septem*ber*, Octo*ber*, Novem*ber*, and Decem*ber*."

I laugh. My drink tastes like Christmas magic and I wonder exactly what Kris put into it. I'm usually a tequila girl, but this is dangerously good.

"Cheers," I say, lifting my cup again. "To you, and me, and the BERs."

"Ho, ho, ho, baby."

I clench my thighs together, aware of the wetness spreading between them. This man drives me feral and I love it. *I love him.*

# three

A Spooktacular Time
<u>Kris</u>

Sabby is hotter than a roaring fire stoked by aged wood and North Pole magic. If it was just me, her, her best friend—Emma, and Emma's boyfriend—who Sabby doesn't know as well as she thinks she does, I could deal.

But *Ray* has locked eyes on her. There're few things as possessive as a wolf.

Our families go back to the 3rd or 4th century. Ray's ancestors knew Errol's too. *Talk about a small world.* I just have to keep him far away from Sabby. My arm loops around her waist and leads her back into the living room. Ray seems to have to gone outside, or maybe he's still milling around the kitchen. It's not important. I do want to hear what Errol has to say about him though.

"I'm going to have sex with Emma and Errol now." Sabby's voice cuts through my thoughts. I blink, taking in the smile across her face followed by the laughter. "Told you he wasn't listening."

"What?" I don't mean to snap, but even I can hear how much of an asshole I sound like. "What did I miss?"

Errol looks at me with something like amused pity. *Fuck, why can't I be good at this?*

"I just lost to both Sabby and Errol that you were in fact listening," Emma says.

"You bet against me?"

Her eyes are wide. She's shorter than Emma, but even more beautiful. Which is saying something, her best friend has almost unnatural beauty.

"I won us a tray of Errol's homemade tortellini and garlic knots," she says. "Since you were off in space, you can't even be mad."

"I should have known when Sabby asked about another man and you didn't even flinch—see, like that!" She points at me and nudges Sabby.

"Huh," my girlfriend says. "I never noticed."

"Told you so," Errol chimes in. "But I can't argue with him. If Emma asked about Ray—"

"Ray?" The name tastes like bile in my mouth.

"And it seems like the right move based on your reaction," she says.

"Now I'm asking too," Emma chimes in.

The music is bumping throughout the house. I'd rather be dancing in the middle of the room than standing off to the side having this conversation, and I *hate* dancing in public. But I did want Errol's insight. I take a gulp of my drink.

"Might as well make it three," I say.

"He's a good kid," Errol says. "His brother's the asshole."

"Pretty sure that apple didn't fall far." I mumble and take another drink, at this rate I'll need a refill soon.

"That's Rey," Errol says. "Ray's brothers are both—"

"Ray's brother's name is Rey?" Emma asks.

"He's one of the three. R-a-y, R-e-y, and Ryan," Errol says.

Sabby rolls her eyes. My mouth drops open and snaps back. "So the werewolf here tonight is—"

"Is Ray," a voice says behind me. "Like a ray of sunshine."

Emma and Errol look around me, Sabby and I turn to face the speaker. He's my height and just as wide.

"Nice to meet you," Sabby says, extending her hand.

I see a warm glow behind his eyes and contemplate breaking his fingers. Not very jolly of me, but I hate how he's looking at her.

"I'm Kris."

Ray's eyes shift to me, the glow's still there. I wonder if Sabby notices. I'm not sure about Emma, I don't even know how much *she* knows about her boyfriend, and I'm not spilling anyone's secrets. Especially not my own.

"We might've met before," he says. "Or maybe our brothers? You have a lot of them, right?"

"I do."

"As Errol said, I have two. One's a bigger asshole than the next."

"You heard all that?" Emma asks. She lifts an eyebrow and raises her hand. "Emma, nice to meet you."

"My partner," Errol says. He waves, bringing Emma in closer.

"Congrats," Ray says.

His eyes drift back to Sabby.

"Kris, my boyfriend," she says.

She's beaming. It'd be cute if it sounded as meaningful as *partner*. Instead it sounds like what we have is trivial, something in a high school romcom. *Fuck, I should have claimed her.* A song starts and before I can figure out what it is both Emma and Sabby have killed their drinks.

"Come on!"

It's hard to tell who shouts over the music.

"Next one," Errol shouts back.

He looks at me. I'm not sure if he's gauging my temperament

or—*shit. What else would he be doing?* The plastic of my cup crinkles as I relax my grip on my cup. I finish it. I turn toward Ray, but he's gone.

"Kris." Errol's voice is flat, his eyes are on the makeshift dance floor.

I follow his gaze.

"Mother fucker," I say. "Fucking wolves."

"Yeah," he says. "But it seems harmless enough."

I glare at him. I don't mean to, but the three of them—Emma, Sabby, and Ray—look too happy dancing around together.

"Is there another reason you hate him?" Errol asks.

"I don't hate him." The plastic on my cup snaps as I make a fist. My eyes meet Errol's. "I hate that he looks at her like that."

"Like he's going to eat her up?"

I throw my head back trying to remember that this is the *partner* of my girlfriend's best friend and that punching him is probably ill-advised.

"I need a drink," I say.

"You're not going to go over there?"

"I'm having a hard enough time not decking you right now."

"Me?!"

His tone is jovial which should calm me down. Except— "You're the one that invited him!"

"Come on," he says, walking toward the kitchen.

He grabs us two drinks and we make our way onto the back deck of Sabby's house. It's just the two of us though.

"So Sabby knows you're a Kringle," Errol says. He takes a sip of his drink and leans against the railing.

I nod. "And Emma?"

"Doesn't." He says.

"Does she know all about your lineage?" Errol nods this time. I ask, "And neither have told the other?"

"Nope," he says. "How'd she take it?"

"Surprisingly well. Emma?"

"A little shell shocked, right as she seemed to adjust, she met my mom."

"Oooff," I say.

"Yeah," he says. "Not the easiest personality, but my dad and my sister like her. I love her, and really, I think that's what counts."

"Fair enough," I say.

Aphrodite is a lot of things, the way Errol described her seems too generous for the stories I've heard. But you can't believe everything. Especially not when it comes to the ancient gods.

"Do you think either of them know he's an actual wolf?"

"Emma should, but probably doesn't." Errol raises his drink toward the door. "What about Sabby?"

"Over the summer she fucked a leprechaun and didn't know."

His drink splashes over the rim as Errol laughs.

"Suck tricky dicks," he says.

"Yeah, well, this one was a female."

He raises his glass again, "The smartest of the bunch."

I nod. Trying to think of anything other than Ray looking at Sabby. There's something in his eyes when he does that bothers me.

"Do you know much about him?"

"Ray?"

I chug half my drink and join Errol against the banister.

"Yeah. As a person," I add.

"I meant what I said, he's a good kid. Works hard. He leads the construction crew I hired for work at the restaurant. Our families have history, but find me two Greeks who don't."

We laugh. Before he can continue, Emma comes stumbling out of the door.

"There you are!"

A light sheen of sweat glistens over her, she's practically

glowing from how radiant she looks. *Aphrodite is going to hate her forever.*

"Hello darling," Errol says, reaching his hand out. "Needed a break?"

"Needed to find you." She glides into his arms and turns to face me. His arms are wrapped around her, together they're a stunning couple. "I'm rooting for you, but if you don't get in there soon you're going to lose your girl."

"That fucking dog—"

"Nope, not the wolf," she says.

I turn to look at her. She's trying to hold back a giggle.

"Christmas," I groan. "Laoise?"

"The leprechaun!" Errol shouts.

"How'd you know?" Emma tilts her head back toward Errol.

"Well, um—"

"Oh, you mean the woman Sabby hooked up with in England was an actual leprechaun?" Neither of us say anything. "I thought all leprechauns were boys."

She makes a face like having an entirely male species would be disgusting. *Definitely impractical.*

"Long story," I say.

"Apparently 8 inches long," Emma says.

"Jesus Christmas!" I roll my eyes, pushing off the wall toward the door, groaning. *First Ray, now Laoise!*

"Leprechauns, gods, werewolves, if any of you see Santa let me know," Emma says.

"Present and accounted for," I say. "And about to make the naughty list." Glass shatters behind me. I stop mid-step. "Halloween costumes," I say. She's frozen in Errol's arms when I face them. Errol's shaking his head. "You meant the costumes."

"You didn't," she says.

"I'm sure Sabby's going to tell you—"

"You're actually *him*?"

"When she's ready. Son of," I say.

"We're going to have a longer talk about this one day," she

says. "But right now you should go get her. When I left they were making a Sabby-sandwich."

Of all the nightmarish things I think about for Halloween, my girlfriend getting double teamed by other people wasn't one of them. I finish my drink and push through the crowd. Emma wasn't kidding. The three of them are the center of the room in a tangle of limbs and hair.

I catch Laoise's eye first. The twinkle to it is mesmerizing and taunting. She knows exactly what she's doing. Her fingers drag along Sabby's body as she turns her attention toward me. My girlfriend sees me and waves.

"KRIS!"

Her voice gets lost in the music, but I know what my name looks like on her lips.

She waves for me to join them, still dancing like her body is hardwired to the music. I weave through the crowd.

"KRIS!" She shouts again. "LAOISE!"

"We finally meet," the leprechaun leans forward, yelling in my ear.

"Can't say it's a pleasure," I say.

She rolls her eyes. Her hand squeezes mine, *Just looking out for her big boy. Wolfie touched her clover.* Her voice echoes in my thoughts.

"Fucking magic," I mumble out loud. I'm not worried about anyone else hearing me, I can hardly hear myself.

I scowl at Ray. That tattoo is on her hip. I drag my eyes down her body until I see it peaking through the strips of leather. I want to break his fingers. I reach forward and Sabby takes my hand, twirling until her ass is pressed against my cock. I don't know how she's grinding to this music, but it doesn't matter. My body responds to hers, moving with her like we're not in a crowd of people.

Nails scratch up my arms sending shivers through my body. I take my eyes off Sabby to see that it's Ray. My eyes move to his face. He looks back at me. There's a hunger in his eyes I can almost taste. *Well, shit,* I think to myself. He raises an eyebrow, I shift my gaze to Sabby as I spin her so her back's now against Ray. I slide myself closer to her, her knees falling on either side of my leg.

Her arms wrap around my neck, pulling me closer. I feel her breath against my ear.

"Emma sent you in?"

I nod. Even though Sabby's between us, I can feel Ray's presence—his nails occasionally scratching my thighs. If she wasn't pressed against me, I'm sure everyone would be able to see my boner.

"Come to claim me?"

"Yes," I say.

"How jealous would you be, watching someone else take me?"

She pulls her face back and I see the smile in her eyes. The naughty little thing she is, trying to goad me. Of course it's fucking working, I'm so hard I'm worried I might bruise her thigh.

"Zabaglione."

Her name slips across my lips in a growl.

"Yes?"

"What did you do?"

My hand wraps around her thigh lifting her up on my leg. She slides down it—I can feel how wet, how hot she is—her ass backs into Ray. He gets closer to her. I watch as she bites her lip moving up and down my thigh. She's dripping, and teasing both of us.

"Red, if you change your mind." The words and her serious tone catch me off guard, but before I can adjust she continues, "it's not what I did."

I lean back so I can see her face. Her eyes are heavy with want, the lids are pulled so low, I wonder if she's going to come just from riding my leg.

"Is my good girl being bad?" I ask.

"Are you going to send me to my room?"

"Bad girls don't get to party, Zabaglione."

She rocks her hips against me. It's slow and torturous. He lets out a low growl. The way she drags her ass up and down Ray's crotch is as exciting as it is frustrating. I'm not sure if I've been more turned on in public.

She shudders, I can feel her pussy tighten against me. "Wolfie or the leprechaun," her tone is different. The neediness in her voice makes my cock twitch. She turns, leans forward, and gives Ray a hug. I can't tell if she said anything to him or not. I look for Laoise—she's in the corner talking to someone dressed like Mr. Clean and the Energizer Bunny had a baby. As Sabby weaves through the living room Ray moves closer to me. We're not grinding with each other, but I can feel the pull of his body.

I swallow. Logic winding its way through my thoughts. I've never picked up a dude before, nor have I had a threesome, which seems to be what Sabby's goal is, *my filthy little slut.* Everything is easy with her. She left me alone to figure this out. My brain short circuits when something cold slides into my hand.

"DRINK!" Emma screams into my ear. I look between her and the plastic cup. "DO IT!"

Her eyes are softer than her command. She points between Ray and Errol, then holds up a finger. Her hands wrap around my wrist and pull me off the makeshift dance floor. Her fingers are like ice from the drink she gave me.

"You look like you're freezing up," she says.

I pound down the sickly sweet liquid, looking over the rim at her.

"What do you mean?" I ask, putting the empty cup down.

"I've known Sabby forever." She says. Her tone makes the jutting hip and crossed arms unnecessary. "We'll all dance and when you're ready just take his hand and lead him upstairs."

"How—"

Three

"FOREVER," she says. "Plus, we came up with the plan together."

She laughs and drags me back to the center where Errol and Ray are dancing. She slides in between us shifting all around until Ray is sandwiched between me and her.

The friction of his jeans against my skin is driving me wild. But not as much as the thought of punishing Sabby for taking both our cocks like a champ. I feel a tingle in my hand as my skin brushes against the light layer of Ray's fur. *Fuck, here goes nothing.*

# four

Howlin' for You
Sabby

If a man kept me waiting this long in the past I would have found a new one. But I know this will be Kris' first threesome and first time with a man in general. We talked about it once when I casually mentioned this one guy Emma and I hooked up with. The guy smelled like Taco Bell, which should have been a turn off, but we were young and there was a lot of tequila.

I'm cleaning up my room, thinking of the conversation. He said he'd be interested. Of course, we hadn't really talked about it since. Stacking my books for the second time since I've been up here, I wonder if I should have followed up. How was I supposed to know that within a ten minute window of dancing with Ray we would have uncovered a list a county road long of things we have in common, including that Kris is the hottest man here, if not in all of the world.

The idea was just a little inkling in my brain when Laoise walked in. Seeing her again, a real person and not some fantasy-fever dream like I had thought she was after our last encounter, it became a real plan.

Four

Either Ray or Laoise would make a great choice, if he decided to do this. Laoise would be in for the sheer mischievousness of it all, and Ray made it clear he'd be down. I think of his body moving against mine. In ripped shorts and no shirt, it was evident how dedicated to his costume he was. Hair covered every exposed part of the man's body. I'm curious if he applied the hair everywhere. I look at the mirror in front of me, surprised to see how pink my cheeks are. I lower my eyebrows and clean up the last of the makeup Emma left in her wake.

I hear the door behind me open. Kris' frame fills the door. The sight steals my breath. He's hotter than any of the characters in Greek mythology, including Hercules. Never would I have thought under that Santa suit was this kind of physique.

"Sabby?" I blink and smile, noticing the shadowy figure behind him. "You're drooling."

Kris steps into the room, a laughing Ray following behind him. I wipe at the corner of my mouth.

"You're ridiculously hot," I say, shrugging.

"You are," Ray says. He takes a step closer to me and Kris closes the door behind him. "But so are you."

I laugh. It's an explosive, manic laugh and I realize the excitement has traveled from between my legs to a full-body nervous kind. This might be Kris' first threesome, but it's the first one I've had without Emma. In the back of my mind I realize she's going to ask a million questions, the thought makes me laugh harder.

"Zabaglione." My breath catches, every part of my body responds to how Kris says my name. In my periphery, I see Ray straighten up a little. "You've been playing games."

Chills break out over my body. My nipples are so hard they press against the furry lining of my bra into the leather. I nod. A low growl comes from Ray. As I shift my weight allowing my thighs to rub together, Kris opens his mouth letting out a single command, "Stop."

I freeze.

Kris walks closer to me, only my eyes follow him until he's

behind me and I can't see him. Ray takes a few steps, and then the two of them are circling me. Kris stops behind me, he's leaning so close I can feel his breath on my ear.

"I gave Ray the safe word too."

The rational part of my brain is relieved. I didn't explain much about our relationship, but when he asked if Kris was "some kind of brute-force sex god," I blushed and bit my lip.

His fingers feel like hot flames on my skin as he pinches my face.

"If you want something to chew on, Zabaglione, you should be on your knees."

I almost drop to the floor, but I don't. I would be good now—Kris' thick cock slamming into the back of my throat—it'll be better when I've pushed him to his limit.

"So she *is* a dirty little slut?"

The question comes from Ray.

Heat builds in my chest. Even under layers of fur and a prosthetic snout, he's attractive. What has my arousal dripping down my leg isn't exactly him—no one but Kris calls me names—it's how tight my boyfriend's grip has become. Hard enough to leave little marks, at last I'm hoping. He's typically restrained when it comes to my face. The only thing harder is his cock pressing into my back.

He lets go. I feel his hand trailing up my thigh.

"What gives you that impression?" Kris asks, licking me from his fingers.

They're both standing in front of me now. My heart is racing like the wolves from Dracula.

"You saw how she was dancing with me before," Ray says.

His voice is deeper than before, strained like he's swallowed a pound of gravel. *Damn.*

"Do you think that's appropriate?" Kris says. "To rub yourself against him like a dog in heat?"

If I was a good girl who listened, I would answer him. Since he kidnapped me and pierced my nipples over the summer I've found it can be so much more fun to not behave. My lips turn up at the corner.

*Whoops, silly me.*

Kris' eyes darken. I'm not sure how it's possible, already the green of his irises are gone. He smirks. Every part of me freezes, that's not what usually happens. Maybe there's a glint or a glimmer of excitement, but he stays in character.

He shouldn't be smiling. And yet… my pussy clenches.

"Was it to make me jealous?" Kris asks. My breath catches in my chest. "Or are you just a dirty little slut as he put it?"

He tilts his head in Ray's direction. I watch as the other man's tongue runs over the sculpted teeth. I wonder if they'll be as sharp as they look against my skin. *I hope so.*

Kris takes another lap around me. His finger grazing my body, but not actually touching it. The man will drive me mental. He stops behind me, each breath he takes forces his muscles to brush against me.

He growls in my ear before he says, "Answer me, Zabaglione."

Chills spread down my arms and back. Kris steps away from me, stopping when he's next to Ray.

"Yes," I say.

His and Ray's eyes widen at my answer.

"Yes what?" Ray asks.

Kris looks over at him, I wonder if Kris is going to stop the game for overstepping. Instead, he smiles again, his gaze shifting back to me.

"Cleverness won't get you out of this one," Kris says, beckoning me over with his finger. I take a step forward. "Since you're nothing more than a dirty, filthy fucking slut, show me." Kris points to Ray. "On him."

Ray laughs as he takes a step closer to me. The heat from his body wraps around me the closer I get. I don't know exactly what Kris wants, or what Ray is comfortable with, I walk around the werewolf, the same way they stalked me. *What would Emma do?* For some, it might be a weird time to think of your best friend, but that bitch always takes the lead in these things knowing damn well I hate being in charge.

I'm completing my first circle around Ray, my fingers running through the fur on his chest. A low growl comes from across the room, when Kris speaks, it stops me in my tracks, "Dance."

I lift my eyes to Ray's. They're staring back at me. They're not the same ones from the living room earlier that were filled with light and a lot of vodka. They're small, narrow and slitted, almost entirely black like shadows instead of actual eyes. They should scream danger.

Instead, I dig my fingers deeper into his fur and wrap my leg around him like he's a pole. I move up and down him, aware of how turned on he is by all of this as well. The hair covering his body tickles. I bite my lip before I can laugh. There's a difference between being a brat and ruining the mood.

I swing around him, this time stopping with my pussy pressed against his torn jeans. I slide down keeping my fingers clenched on his belt, and pop my ass into the air. Kris should enjoy the view since my skirt is more shreds than actual fabric. The buckle is easy enough to get off while I'm shaking my ass.

Ray's pants drop to the floor and I spin myself around to back up onto him. It doesn't feel like he had anything on underneath, and I'm bummed I didn't look. Kris is glaring from across the room. I find it motivating. I twist my body around, lifting my leg around Ray's frame. His lower body is covered in fur, but it's shorter. I figure it's his.

He is hard and long. I feel him poking me as I grind his thigh. Ray makes a low guttural noise as he wraps his hands under my ass shifting me closer to him. I dip backwards, aware of Ray's eyes traveling down my neck to my breasts. Kris is sitting in my chair, the one Emma did my makeup on earlier. I unbuckle the bralette letting it slide off my arms.

My nipples are pert and the center of Kris' attention. I pull myself up wrapping one of my arms around Ray letting the other travel down his body. We're moving slower, each thrust deliberate. When my hand slips between us, I wrap it around his girth.

Sliding down his body again, I kneel in front of him. The hand that was behind his head is now tweaking his nipples. Little snarls of pleasure escape him.

"Sabby," Kris says. It's a warning. I keep running my hand over Ray's length. "You're not a tease."

If I wasn't already soaked, his tone would have gotten me there. I angle myself so I can see Kris in my periphery, and reach for Ray's cock with my tongue. I graze the tip of it.

"She's being one now," Ray says, his voice a rumble.

"She knows better than that, don't you Zabaglione?"

I swallow and wrap my lips around Ray. He hisses and I gather my hair behind me and work my way up and down his shaft. Each time I take more of him into my mouth until I gag. Tears reach my eyes, but I keep going. My eyes cut over to Kris. I see enough of him to know his own hand is mimicking what I'm doing for Ray.

I can feel how wet I am; seeing Kris watching, hearing Ray every time he hits the back of my throat. I knead Ray's balls trying to keep my hands off my own clit. I clench my thighs together, aching for any relief.

"Spread your legs," Kris says.

*Fuck.*

I'm swirling my tongue around the head of Ray's cock as I stroke him. I can feel his balls tighten. I bring my mouth down to the base, my fingers digging into his thighs.

"Slower."

I can't tell who the command comes from. I listen, his cock leaves my mouth with a pop. Strings of salvia hang from my lips, still on him.

A finger swipes through my wetness and I moan. Kris reaches in front of me and slides his finger into my mouth. I can taste my arousal on him. He does it again. This time I shudder as he teases my clit for a moment. I look up, Ray licks me off of Kris, taking his whole digit into the back of his throat.

Kris's cock twitches in front of me. Their tips are so close together. I lean forward and run my tongue between them. The familiar taste of Kris' pre-cum makes me moan. I use both my hands pumping them into my mouth. The small rocks my body makes with each move send a deeper level of want through me.

My pussy is heavy, I need to be filled soon. Through hooded eyelids I watch as Kris replaces his finger with his tongue.

"Fuck." The word is muffled as I'm trying to get them both into my mouth. "Please."

Even as their kiss breaks, my tongue is unrelenting.

"She's begging for it," Ray says.

"She doesn't even know what she's begging for" Kris says.

I'm in so much trouble, the thought makes me moan.

Ray reaches down and throws me over his shoulder like a sack of potatoes. I have a great view of his ass. Even in full werewolf hair costume, it's bitable. I yelp as he tosses me onto the bed. I bounce and see Kris' legs are on both sides of me. He's completely naked.

I want to kiss every part of him. Starting at his knee, I lick my way up to his massive cock standing at attention like it was waiting for me. My insides are raging with desire. I impale myself on him gagging as he cuts off all of my air supply. I'm moving up and down, spit pooling around the base. I shudder as I feel a tongue run up the crack of my ass.

Ray growls in my ear as he works his knuckle in a small circle around the tight muscle. I arch my back pushing against him as I continue to choke myself on Kris. I groan as Ray increases the pressure. I buck myself against him, forcing him to increase his speed. Kris tugs on his cock, I suck trying to keep him inside, but lose.

He flops it against my face. I turn giving him better access. He slaps me with it, the wet sound drives me wild. Ray is on the side of my bed. Half hunched, half standing—his fingers work my tight hole as Kris strokes him. He leans in and licks my face. I arch back, each man's hand finds the barbells decorating my nipples. One twists, where the other pulls. The room fades to black as the sensations run through me. I shiver, aware of my arousal soaking my thighs, the bed.

I bend back down taking Kris into my mouth again. He's still jerking Ray off, I try to match the pace, I'm desperate for more.

"Please!"

My cries are muffled. Kris takes his hand from my breast and slides it between my thighs, pinching at the little bean of nerves, while Ray—still teasing my asshole—slips a finger into my pussy.

It sounds like rainwater splashing onto the sidewalk. With my release dripping over their fingers, Kris slips them into Ray's mouth while he plunges the digit fully into my ass. I'm not sure whose groans are whose. I'm practically feral riding Ray's hand, wishing for either one of them to be deep inside me.

"You think she's learned?"

Kris' voice is husky. He sounds just as delirious with want as I am.

"How teasing is mean?" Ray asks.

"Yeah." Kris takes his hands back from Ray's cock—I can see the veins pulsing from here—and Ray's mouth, and places them on my hips. Lifting me up he positions the tip, shiny from my spit, at my slit. He teases the small bud again as Ray removes his fingers—I whimper at the emptiness—replacing it with his head of his penis against my entrance. "You've been such a dirty little slut, Zabaglione. Do you think you can take both of us at once?"

I howl as they shift inside me. I've never been more filled in my whole life. All I can do is gasp.

"That's a good girl," Ray says.

The tips of his nails bring goosebumps up my arm as he pets it.

"Can you take all of us?" Kris asks. His fingers are circling my hip bones. I feel my walls clench around him. I'm falling over the edge with each of their strokes. "Zabaglione?"

"Yes." My voice is a whisper.

Then they slide in further. It feels like *too* much. Kris works one of my nipples and my clit. I catch my breath, and let out a moan. Ray goes for my other nipple, kissing my neck. The prickle of his teeth is intoxicating. So many sensations, I feel myself gushing over Kris' cock.

"Yes, you fucking slut." He growls, "Come all over me."

"Oh God," Ray says, his voice breathless.

"You like when my good girl comes on you?" Kris asks Ray.

"Yes." His voice is strained.

They're both tugging at my nipple now, sending waves of pleasure through me.

"I can feel you throbbing inside her," Kris says. Ray drops his head onto mine. They're both so much taller than me. Kris pushes himself up. He kisses my lips, nose, and forehead giving me a wink only I can see. Then he tilts his face upward. I watch as Ray's tongue slips between Kris' teeth. I rock my body adjusting to their sizes, the fullness of it all. Kris pulls back and looks into my eyes, "You can take the rest."

It's not a question. He knows my body, knows how I like it. A shiver rips through my body and then they're both fully seated in me. Their hard bodies sandwiching me. I'm not sure I'm holding myself up any more. It doesn't matter, I'm ready and I need all of them.

"Fuck me, please!" I scream.

They separate, Kris laying down, Ray straight behind me. They find a rhythm. Kris pounding my pussy as Ray rides my ass. I can feel them both, impossibly hard, driving into me.

"Kris." My boyfriend's name from Ray's lips does something to me. I'm already teetering so close. "Sabby, are you ready?"

I push back against Ray, the angle deepens how far Kris goes and I swear the man is rearranging my chest cavity.

"Oh god, oh god," he grunts, rutting harder against me.

Kris runs his thumb over my clit and I come undone, "Hol-holy-ho-holy shit." Ray holds onto my body as I shake. "Santa Daddy?"

He hasn't come yet. I can feel Ray spasming inside me, still so hard. Kris is still going.

"Not yet, Zabaglione." His eyes shift from me to Ray. I can't hold mine open anymore. "You think you have more in you, Ray?"

"I nutted, I didn't knot."

"Didn't think so," Kris says.

Their words float above me. Everything is vibrating around me and it feels like my soul is hanging above my body.

The room spins. I open my eyes to see my bed. Ray is standing up. His cock is hard, jutted up toward the ceiling. Kris rolls off the bed and moves behind me. I look to see Ray laying where Kris had been before. My brain is stuck in slow motion, while the rest of me is tingling.

"Sit," Kris says. I plop back onto my heels. "No, Zabaglione." He leans forward, his breath tickling my ear. "On his cock." I raise my eyebrow at him. "Turn and face Ray." I do, my body feels like chopped up jelly, but I manage. "Now sit your tight asshole on his cock like the good slut you are."

I moan. *Yes*, I think, the words trapped somewhere in my throat. I push myself up, smile at Ray and ease his penis into my ass inch by inch. I can feel Kris stroking himself behind me. The movement of air, the occasional nudge of his hand. He's watching with want. I gasp—the feeling, being watched—it's intoxicating.

"I'm going to fuck you now," Kris says. "And my girl will splash all over you, you dirty beast."

Ray's cock twitches inside me. Without some kind of touch it feels like too much. I open my mouth to tell Kris, as his hand makes slow circles around my swollen clit.

"Kris!" Ray and I groan at the same time.

I watch as Ray's eyes widen and then disappear behind

hooded lids as my boyfriend slides into Ray's ass. At least that's what I assume, I can only see Ray's face and feel his body move with whatever Kris is doing to him.

Ray opens his eyes looking at both of us. I don't have to wonder what he sees. As he pinches my nipple with one hand, his other cupping my pussy, he says, "You two are fucking hot." He flexes his fingers, slipping two inside.

His name slips through my lips, "Ray." We're moving slower this time. Ray easing deeper and deeper in my ass. Kris' body moves with mine, still teasing my clit, now the other nipple.

Ray takes over my nipples, pumping a little faster inside me. Kris's body rocks against mine, his hand angled inside me.

"I'm gonna—"

Kris works his fingers and I splash over Ray's body. My eyes roll back into my head and I can feel Ray filling me up. He feels even bigger than he was before. We're both howling like wolves. I'm giving myself over to every sensation. Kris grunting behind me. My body slumps backwards resting against Kris. He hugs me. His heart pounds underneath my head. I shiver and feel my eyes get heavier.

The last thing I hear is Kris saying, "Such a good girl, Sabby."

# five

Howl at the Moon
<u>Kris</u>

I don't often use my special North Pole touch on Sabby, but given that there's a werewolf knotted inside her, I think it's a good exception.

"Hold her up?" I ask Ray.

I slide my cock out, and run over to the bathroom to grab a damp towel and a dry one. Giving myself a quick wash up I replay what we did, surprised to be a little chubbed up. If all threesomes are like that, I've been missing out.

In my heart I know it wouldn't be the same without Sabby. That woman makes me fearless and so incredibly horny. There's no doubt that I love her. I walk back in the room. Ray is studying Sabby's face. Where I would usually be jealous, I can appreciate his knowledge of the magical.

"So is she sleeping or just. . ." his voice trails off.

"Sleeping, kind of. It'll be like we hit pause. She won't know the difference really." He raises an eyebrow at me. "Of course I'm going to tell her. Just wasn't sure about the werewolf thing yet."

"Kris," Ray says. He juts his chin toward Sabby's hips. "She got fucked by a leprechaun. One who I'm pretty sure is downstairs."

I roll my eyes. "Fucking Laoise."

He laughs, letting out a gasp as the warm towel cleans between his legs.

"So you guys do this often?"

"Nope." I say. "You're the first one."

I gather Sabby's hair and throw it over her one shoulder. She hates when it sticks to the back of her neck.

"I wouldn't have known," he says. "Have you ever been with a man before?"

I shake my head, taking a seat behind Sabby. Ray eases her back onto my body. The silence that fills the room is comfortable. I feel bad about earlier.

"I shouldn't't've stared you down before," I say.

"You had me confused with one of my brothers," he says. "Trust me, I get it."

"That and the way you were looking at her—"

His laughter shakes the bed.

"I wasn't—" I open my mouth to protest, but Ray continues, "Okay, I was. But I was looking at both of you."

I feel the color rising to my cheeks.

"Well, thanks, I guess." He chuckles and this time I join him. "So how long will you stay like that?"

"Knotted?"

"Yeah."

"Five minutes to a half hour. It'd be quicker if you weren't hot and just sitting there like a carved statue."

"You want me to, uh—" I don't really know the word for it. I've only ever tried it on myself. "Do you trust me?"

"Yeah." He laughs again.

I rub my hands together thinking every calming thought I can while envisioning a snowball. A faint blue light glows between them and I lean down, reaching under Sabby, and grab both of Ray's nuts.

He shivers. I watch as his cock drops a little. He's still in her, but he'll be able to pull out now. I get in position and wake Sabby up. She yawns and stretches back onto me.

"Damn," she says. "You two could wreck a girl."

We both laugh.

"You can do your own damage," Ray says.

"You don't know the half of it," I laugh. "Let's go get you cleaned up. Then the three of us will head back down to the party?"

"Sounds good!"

* * *

We're all cleaned up, Ray is heading downstairs in his costume, but Sabby and I have opted for matching Halloween pjs I brought with me as a surprise. We're walking past the guest room when we all stop.

"Laoise! Osterhase!" Emma's voice is clear as day. "Errol! Oh god!"

I look between Ray and Sabby, "Seems we're not the only ones to have a little extra fun tonight."

Sabby's head is swiveling between the two of us. "Why do I have a feeling you two know more than you're saying?"

"I know nothing," Ray says, laughing.

"You do!" She turns toward me, "and you?"

"I'll tell you when you're older!"

I run off with Ray through the party and into the kitchen for more drinks. It's Sabby's favorite time of the year, and when she's happy, I'm happy.

# playlist

Trick-or-Treat Playlist
*(Please note: I do not own the rights to these songs, I just love them—*
*esp for a cryptid threesome)*

- Walter Murphy by A Fifth of Beethoven
- Monster Mash Cover by Leo Moracchioli
- Werewolves of London by Warren Devon
- I Was A Teenage Werewolf by The Cramps
- Black No. 1 by Type O Negative
- Mommy, Can I Go Out & Kill Tonight? by Misfits
- Halloween (She's So Mean) by Rob Zombie
- Dig Up Her Bones by Misfits
- Living Dead Girl by Rob Zombie
- Hungry Like the Wolf by Duran Duran
- Feed My Frankenstein by Alice Cooper
- Psycho Killer by Talking Heads
- 197666 by Murderdolls
- Full Tilt Boogie by Uncle Louie (feat. Walter Murphy)
- Dead Man's Party by Oingo Boingo
- (Don't Fear) The Reaper by Blue Öyster Cult
- War Pigs/Luke's Wall by Black Sabbath

Playlist

- Runnin' with the Devil by Van Halen
- Siouxsie and The Banshees by Spellbound
- Bela Lugosi's Dead by Bauhaus
- What's Inside a Girl by The Cramps
- Take it Like a Man by KMFDM
- Duality by Slipknot

# afterword

Since you've been *such a good reader*... here's a treat!

Santa Daddy, Cupid's Angel, and Luck Be a Leprechaun are now available on Audible. Written by me, Libby Scores, narrated by Meg Sylvan.

# about the author

Libby Scores is a lot of things, including a writer of smut. To learn more about her and the rest of the holiday series of naught novellas: https://www.elizabethscozzari.com/

Thank you for reading!!!